the view from the moon.

julianna marie

Copyright ©2020 by Julianna Marie

All rights reserved. No part of this book may be reproduced in any form on by an electronic or mechanical means, including information storage and retrieval systems, without permission in writing from the publisher, except by a reviewer who may quote brief passages in a review.

to those who are lost,
stuck on the moon and in space:
you are not alone.

the view of the moon

she packed her bags full of trust
and filled her mind with the notion
that greater things lay
with the "stars..."

and the city full of them.

oz is sean kingston and palm trees

three tornadoes of hair
driving down the p.c.h
holding credit cards with their last name
but their parent's first,
laughing behind designer knockoff sunglasses
to a song called "beautiful girls."

she looked out of the tinted windows
and realized she had never lived under a sky
with so many palm trees
and with a sun so blindingly bright.

in california, every road is paved
with a yellow-bricked haze
that makes you forget
that kansas may be your home,
but "daddy's audi" is your ruby slipper,

and oz is sean kingston and palm trees.

los angeles is a garden

she was surrounded by flowers,
vibrant petals and tall, skinny stems
with full, developed leaves
and well-pollinated centers.

and she couldn't help but to feel judged
for her wilted petals and short, fat stems
with lacking leaves
and a center that left much to be
desired.

driving home after saying goodbye

one limp hand on the wheel,
the other hanging numbly by my side
as the streetlights become hazy
and blur with each melancholy memory
that rolls down my cheeks.

"can i get pulled over
for driving under the speed limit?"
i ask myself as my aching heart
stops my foot from pressing the gas.

and my mind begins to wander,
and i begin to wonder
if i'll ever drive on the other side
of the road ever again.

november 10th, laguna beach

we ate overpriced toast
and coffees with art stenciled onto them,
not caring about if the parking meter was paid for
because at least we had scraped up enough money
to pay for breakfast.

then we walked to the beach
weaving through trinket shops
with branded beach apparel,
until we were finally able to freeze our asses off
in the november pacific
and laugh about,
after a while,
if it was even cold anymore.

and i remember how i felt after all of that:
the (shitty) toast,
trinkets,
and frozen water
as we drove through the sunset-lit hills.

i felt,
for the first time in months,
happy.

black and blue for you

i want to be with you
until my back
is black and blue
from simply doing nothing
all day.

j.r.

bob dylan car rides
in a silver subaru with the windows down,
surrounded by the sand, the ocean, and palm trees,
driving to the first tattoo parlor we could find.

it was these stupid adventures,
that made you feel like family.

come over

bon iver sounds more melancholy
whenever i lie down without your warmth
as my second blanket.

the further you are from me,
the closer i feel to the moon.
because without you beside me
i feel like the stars are much closer
than your body.

so i guess what i'm trying to say,
without my poetic bullshit, is
come over.

angela

my mom is strong like
a storm and beautiful like
the springtime flowers.

september, huntington beach, a puka shell bracelet.

nothing made me happier
than the beach days
turned
party nights:
memories i would solidify
as a bracelet on my right wrist
like i do with all of my
favorite moments.

i often wonder
if i judge things too soon,
and buy bracelets too carelessly
without realizing that
even if i take my bracelet
off,
a faint tan line will always
remain.

i guess what i'm trying to say is:
moments will leave marks on you
forever.

so beware of the bracelets
you choose to buy.

bonding through the bad

i remember every night feeling like a sleepover:
we'd talk about boys and secrets and
our fucked-up lives,
and bonding through the bad,
and cry because both of us finally felt
so much less alone.

routine

a ray of light through half-opened blinds,
a haze of last night in the air.
smudged makeup on
wrinkled sheets
and clothes that smell like bonfires.

a pair of shoes
caked with dying grass,
a passed out student with a lost student id,
next to left-over munchies on the floor.

a curl in my stomach,
a hammer in my head,
stale clothes on my body,
and vodka in my aura,

i roll out of bed,
just to do it all again.

growing pains

do you remember how easy it was being sixteen?
it felt like the nights were longer
and the lights were brighter
and *fuck*,
even the food tasted better
because it only came with flavor,
and no consequential calories.

your words were sweeter then.
they felt like fresh blankets from the dryer and
tasted like fresh honey.

but blankets cool,
and even honey expires.

and the sun had to rise,
and the lights had to dim,
and the days had to end,
because we eventually had to turn seventeen.
and too much honey
can give you cavities.

but i still don't know why
as soon as you're not sixteen anymore
the food tastes different
and goes straight to your thighs.

california sunset

i want to live life
under skies of orange and pink,
and
i want to run barefoot without ever stopping to think
about how i could step on
glass
at any second.

i want to live life
in a beautifully ignorant mindset
and i want to live life
dancing under a california sunset.

mac demarco in los angeles

under a starry los angeles sky,
in the nosebleeds of the greek,
i remember thinking to myself:
"this is the best 35 dollars
we have ever spent."

and i knew you all agreed
as we took poor quality iphone videos
and freaked out the nighborhood
dancing around in IPA scented air
to "salad days" and "my kind of woman"
and not even caring that it was a school night
and not even caring that the drive home was an hour long
because at least we could see how the freeways look when they're empty
and how the los angeles skyline looks friendlier
at nighttime.

it might've been the beer,
but i think
that was the first time i saw stars in los angeles.

and i had hoped that it wouldn't be the last.

letters

i want to be written about
on coffee-stained notebook papers
with the ripped edges still attached.

and i want to be described
in romance languages
set to the tune of an acoustic love song.

i want to be the thing
that fills the ruled-lines of your mind
with metaphors and imagery,
but never hyperbole.

and i want those letters
to be tucked away for me to find
when i look for the papers
that i write on about you.

> *-please, just rip the edges off of the paper*
> *next time*

textbook

i hate the way you think of her
more than you think of me,
and the way she always seems to come up
during our candlelit conversations.

i hate her spiral-bound spine
and the fact that it's stronger than mine.
and the fact she knows more than me.
and the way you can learn more from her
than you could ever learn from me.

and i hate the way you talk about her,
the fact that your family is proud of her
and how she makes you better in ways that i never could.

i hate her complexity.
her perfection.
her numbered pages of proofread excellence
and how she'll always know what to say.

i hate how she took my framed photo's spot
on your bookshelf,
and how you cancel dates to stay up in the library with her
until the stars walk you home.

i hate how easy it was to leave me for her.

i hate the no matter how hard i try,
i will never be as important.

and i hate that,
deep down,
i know she's better for you anyway.

mirror, mirror

"mirror, mirror on the wall,
who is the fairest one of all?

is it me?"
i ask as i cover my growling stomach
with trauma-stained arms
and hollowed eyes.

because it's so hard to feel beautiful
while you look in a mirror with bias,
that has memorized your flaws like flashcards
with highlighted insecurities.

the mirror will never be fair,
so i guess
neither will i.

our song

when i was fifteen,
i showed you a song that reminded me
of you.

you probably don't remember,
i showed you lots of songs,
and it was probably just white noise
while you focused on the road.

when i was sixteen,
i showed it to you again.
you smiled.
so did i.

when i was seventeen,
i was too busy to show it to you.
but as we sat in the back of your car,
looking at the stars through tinted windows,
you showed it to
me,
and my stomach filled with shooting stars
because i was sure you'd forgotten it.

and now i'm eighteen,
and i haven't heard that song in months
because my heart screams at each plucking string,
and tears form at each chord and fall with every lyric.

and my heart breaks when i think of
the backseats of cars,
and shooting stars,
and all of the things that made that song
ours.

and i hope that next year,
even if i have forgotten the melody,
that you'll be the one to show it to me
and remind me
of our song.

and i hope that next year,
even if i have forgotten the melody,
that you'll be the one to show it to me
and remind me of our song.

i've changed (i think)

i'm not the same girl i was when you met me.

and i think that's a good thing...
right?

tsunami

it comes in waves.

the first thing that happens is you start to lose feeling in your fingertips: that uncomfortable tingling sensation that usually happens whenever your foot stays still for two long. it feels like every induvidual cell and atom in your fingers are sewing needles, pinging off of each other and fighting feverishly.

then you start to sweat. and you don't know why because you're in an airconditioned room that would otherwise make your hair stand up and your skin raise. and you sweat until your mouth becomes dry and until there's an invisible weight on your chest that you don't have the strength to lift.

you struggle to breathe and stifle your sweat until the tsunami breaks down those emotional barriers you fight every day to control. the floodgates break and the dams overflow until you're completely swallowed into a sea of lost control and surpression. and you're drowning. and for those few moments, it feels like nothing and nobody can pull you out of the water. your chest tightens and your breathing quickens and you just can't
stop
crying
and
feeling
every emotion and every feeling and every sense all at once. and every second feels like an hour and every minute feels like a lifetime until the waves pass and the ocean calms until the tide rises again.

and, because of this, every day feels like some sort of fight to some sort of surface that i will never, *ever* be able to swim to.

flashback, 2018, party favor.

confetti kisses, minty-fresh years. new years eve was always the same:

the clock strikes
midnight, your hands on my hips and your lips touching mine as storms of champagne shake and brew.

the streamers that streak the wall will wilt as hours pass, and we lose ourselves with every
celebratory, burning shot lined up on the counter. the room is filled with a golden haze, smiles like diamonds glistening in the light.

new years eve, with you, was always the same. our confetti kisses, our minty-fresh year.

ten.

but one extra party favor, the one i saved just for you, sits alone on the counter, a cardboard island in a sea of stained wood. i stare at it through the glimmering smiles, hoping each doorbell ring will come from your fingertips.

nine.

i am surrounded by smiles, but mine is fictitious.

eight.

the year begins to close, like the door you slammed before you left. confetti kisses fading, minty-fresh years losing their crisp.

seven.

and now there is no golden haze, and the shots on the counter taste like clear water. they're no longer for celebration, alcoholic anesthetics cure a broken year's end.

six.

the party favor i saved lays on the ground, damp from show's wet snow. i want to put it back up, smile and pretend. you're on your way. you're always late.

five.

two more shots. they burn less the less i think.

four.

the ball on the television lines up to drop. his hands are on her hips. her lips pucker into his. i look through the fading golden haze.

it's you..

three.

i step over the wilting party favor. the haze slowly grows warmer with each step i take.

two.

i feel the shots burning in the back of my throat as i realize,

one.

you had never come back at all. and i feel the champagne storms brewing as confetti kisses surround me. the stale taste of the new year sticks in my mouth.

happy new year.

before

the sky has been blue for far too long,

i'm just wondering if it'll ever rain again.

seratonin shots

oversized sweatshirts with a stale party smell:
vodka, the official colliagiate perfume.

with a pounding head,
i reapply my dull eyeliner
and strip my hair with heat damage
because pretty girls have straight hair.

shot after shot,
artificial seratonin down my throat,
i hide under flashing lights
from men that will only care about a girl
for three minutes, if she's lucky.

this is what happiness looks like.

until seratonin ends up in the toilet
of a bathroom i've never even seen.
and i think about texting the one man
who still cares.

i didn't know that these shots
lasted less than a frat boy,
and i didn't know that without them,
i would realize

this isn't what happiness looks like.

do you like when it rains?

do you like when it rains?
when wet pieces of the stars fall
and splash galaxies onto the pavement,
and the way the droplets dance
to pitter-patter songs
with lyrics that make you think?

and when you think,
do you think of me?

do you wonder if the rain falls
in parallel patterns to mine?
or if our droplets dance to the same song,
keeping perfect time?

i hope you like when it rains,
but i hope you like when it stops, too.
when yellow rays peek out from grey clouds
and the birds take over the melody of the rain's song.

i hope you still think of me
after the rain is gone.

best (?) of both worlds

when i was younger, i watched hannah montana and thought "it would be so frikkin' cool to live a double life like miley stewart (cyrus?) and be a different person when i'm at school but also a different person whenever i'm alone." granted, being a teenage girl by day and an international popstar by night (even at age twenty) is totally kickass and a completely reasonable thing to think is cool.

but then i grew up. and while i didn't become an "international popstar" with an obviously fake blonde wig, i started to live a double life. a duel reality that i created without even knowing: skipping class and partying to drown out my problems at one moment, but listening to folk music and writing poetry and secretly enjoying the film class that everyone around me hated, and being upset that i didn't go to that class yesterday.

the thing that hannah montana didn't show me was how easy it was to fully lose your identity when you're split between two entirely different worlds. without even realizing, you're sucked into believing that this flase life, this false identity, was who you were all along.

and i wish hannah would've illustrated that better before telling me that i'd have the "best of both worlds" when it was obvious that i no longer had anything of either.

lightyears

why do you keep asking me to stay while all you do is keep me at bay?

and why does it feel like each day, you grow another lightyear away?

losing my religion

is it god?
or just the way the
light shines through the blinds?

thanksgiving break, 2018

i was scared to see you again because i was so scared that you would notice that i gained weight or the fact that my hair was dark and short but you always said it looked pretty whenever it was natural and long. that's part of the reason why i wanted to cut it whenever we broke up. distancing myself from you by stripping myself of the things you loved, was easy.

but when i got into your car, seeing you for the first time in three months and being just your friend instead of your person for the first time in three years, i wasn't scared if you didn't like my hair or my newly grown tummy.

i was scared that you didn't feel the same way i felt whenever i saw you again. and i was scared because i realized that i was still in love with someone who i wasn't sure loved me back anymore.

how i feel

"i feel so alone"
i think as i'm surrounded
by other people.

maybe if i just smile,
i'll finally feel better

pity poem

i don't want pity
or a pat on my back,
an "im sorry" clouded in discomfort
and accidental insincerity.

i want someone
to nod silently
then hug me so tightly that my tears spill out,
or someone to write about my words
in their journal
and tell their friends that someone finally gets it.

i don't want pity.
i want to be understood.

do the stars still shine in california?

tonight
it's just me and the stars
sharing moondust covered secrets
in the city that knows everything about everyone.

do the stars still shine in california?
because i can still see the,
amongst the artificial lights
that dull the authentic glow.

and i hope they notice how badly i want to
shine.
for i am a candle
in a sea of stadium lights.

but tonight,
i'll look up at the stars only i can see
and beg them not to forget me
and i'll do the same.

s.f, b.m, k.z, s.m, s.c.

they were sprouted from similar soil as me,
but grew into different flowers
that i took for granted
when i was woo'ed by silk flowers
in plastic, foreign soil.

red

our friendship was unexpected
but magnetic,
i guess opposites attract.

i listened to your stories
over fast food feasts
until the sunrise peeked through our blinds.
and i showed you parts of myself
that i never even knew i had
in sacred, sunset painted places
on adventures ill never forget.

red-string friendship bracelets,
liquor bottles with red caps
that tasted like cinnamon,
singing at red lights
in your boyfriends car,
red wine stains on the bathroom walls
and tucked into closets.

i saw friendship in all things
red,
but ignored the red flags
because i guess they just seemed to blend in.

and now i wonder,
red face with embarrassment,
if we were ever friends at all
and if you ever even liked the color red at all.

the girl in my mirror

today i looked in the mirror
and barely recognized
the girl in it.

her perfectly lipstick-ed lips
hissed insults,
harsh words that dripped
out of her mouth
and cut my skin.
her eyeliner smeared eyes
pierced me with judgement
and lacked that familiar spark
of liveliness.

i didn't recognize
the dark circles
of empathy
under her eyes,
pleading for peace,
for sleep,
for someone to understand.

so i asked her,
"who are you"
and she said back to me,
"what you've made me
become."

i still love you after the pain.

there are so many things (i) could say,
but i (still) can't find the words.

is it okay to (love you)?
even (after) what you did?
even after (the pain) you caused?

after

it rained today.
and i never thought i'd say
that i missed when skies were blue.

on the moon

she looked at the sky
with a smile
and a glimmer in her eye,
and promised herself that someday soon,
she would travel through space
and land on the moon.

i wish someone could've told me
how, up here, isolation
does not make you free,
and that being on the moon
isn't all it's cracked up to be.

companionship

my only companion
is the stale smoke from a blunt
i didn't smoke

and i have never felt so alone.

remedy

maybe it i drink enough tonight,
the burning of my throat
will overpower the sting i constantly feel
as i salt my own wounds.

sixteen

i long for the simplicity
that i called complexity,
and i long for the naivety
that i bragged didn't exist
even though it did.

hindsight

i should've known
when our friendship bracelet broke off of your wrist
in front of my eyes,
and you didn't even stoop down
to pick up the pieces.

mom and dad

they're right when they say, "you never realize how good you have it until it's gone." and i realized this whenever i got sick for the first time laying in a dorm bed across the county from the two people who cared about me more than they cared about anyone else. my dad wasn't there to pick me up ginger ale and watch a funny movie with me because, in his eyes, laughter can quite literally cure anything. and my mom wasn't there to take my temperature and make sure that i was drinking enough fluids because she has that instinct to take care of everyone, sometimes even before she takes care of herself.

and even though my cold passed and i went on with my life, i still missed watching cooking shows with my dad and critiquing the professional chefs while we could barely cook toast and i still missed eating cheese fries and plain double cheeseburgers while gossiping with my mom after strolling through target and not buying anything.

because while you may be an "adult," you're still a kid as long as your parents are there. and when you suddenly have to buck up and live life without them, you can't help but to feel so, entirely helpless.

never take them for granted.

broken bits

maybe the reason i feel so awful
is because i give all the good pieces of myself to others

and i'm stuck to live
with the broken bits.

1.26.19

from up here,
the stars are within my reach
but yet,
the moon is too far.

and i feel no pain
when i look at the sky above me,
but even more so when i look at the ground below.

i have never seen the earth
look so peaceful,
the way the streetlights look like
their very own versions of stars.

it's so far down,
but it's so peaceful
and i want to dip my toes in,
then jump all together,

maybe then
i can finally touch the moon.

if i evaporate

like morning dew on grass,
it's almost as if i could vanish into the
sky
without anyone realizing that i was even there
at all.

dishrag

i'm cold and damp,
but throw me into hot water
and stifle my movement
with a rigid grip.

and wring me out,
with the final pieces of me
spiraling down into the drain.

hang me out to dry,
only to use me again once your hands
get dirty.

read receipts

hey
heyyy
are u awake
please wake
up
im so ducking sad
*fucking

can we just have one more jnight where we talk to eachother like we
used to
heyyy
i think i drank too . much
i miss you
pleasde wake up

read 2:23am

through instagram filtered glasses

they only ask me what it's like
to live in the city
of palm tree painted skies and
70 degree air.
and ask me if it's as cool as it looks in the movies
or on the instagram feed that only serves to feed
their hunger to hear the stories
of those people in those movies.

but they rarely ask about me,
and how it must feel to live in a city
that most of them have only visited in idealistic daydreams of
palm tree painted skies
with permanent instagram filters
that make the sky look bluer
than it ever actually was.

they never ask me if i miss the stars
or the way people tip 20% even if i got the order wrong.
the way people never judge you
if you're larger than a size two
and the way midwest skies don't need instagram filters
to be so fucking blue.

but instead i'll tell them that through the palm trees
i can still see the stars,
and tell them that one celebrity was so generous
even though i watched them stiff their waiter

because i'm so afraid to let them know
how alone
this place feels without fixing the hue and saturation,
and let them think this grass is greener than their grass is,
and let them see my life
though instagram filtered glasses.

curing a broken heart

nothing can cure a broken heart
like sleepless nights
and flashing lights
and clear liquid that burns
not only your throat
but the realizations that
this is not who you are.

suffocated in false realities
and burried in lies,
i convince myself that
if i inject myself with poison,
i would no longer feel pain.

but after a while,
even the numbest of people ache to feel something.

even if it's pain.

why she hated prom

lipstick on a pig,
a sausage stuffed in white, polyester casing.

her mirror told lies
that she had no choice but to believe.

floating

each day i feel like
gravity is pulling me
further and further from reality
until i am aimlessly floating in
negative
space,
with no clue
as to how i got here
in the first place.

numb – a haiku.

i'm so fucking numb,
i've forgotten what feeling
would even feel like.

bul(l shit)imia

i stuck my fingers
down my throat to eject the
pain i was force-fed.

voodoo doll

if you were
to punch someone's shoulder,
i would get a bruise instead.
and if you were
to hurt them with words
those words would show up on my mind.
and if you were
to cut their skin,
i would bleed twice as much
as they would've.

cycles

i find myself in a constant cycle of
hurt.
maybe it's because
i'm a masochist
or maybe i just simply forgive
too easily.

same thing either way.

a trade

she had long brown hair
with golden highlights
and a sunny disposition.
but when she met
them,
she dyed her hair black and said,
"fuck it, this is who i am."

she hid her love for books
under cheap booze,
and traded her passion for life
for things that would end it.

she left coffee shops with people who listened
for smoke-filled rooms with people who didn't care.

and when people said she looked different,
it took her all her strength to pretend
that this is just who she was.

but in reality,
she traded her hair and her smile
for temporary acceptance
and permanent abandonment.

before the shower thoughts.

i don't know why i look at myself before i shower. i never like what i see. i never like to see hunched over shoulders and a permanent maternal stomach. i never like to look at the way my thighs touch and the way my hips seem to grow bigger and bigger with each day. i never like to see how my boobs are unlovable and the forever lumps on my ass that tell me perfection is unattainable.

i never like to see the red blotches of where i pinch my skin and squish my fat. i never like to see the way my ribs punch through my skin before they evaporate before my eyes. i never like to see the uncontrollable things i've been taught to despise and the thousands of things i would change if i only had time.

i never like to see the body i hate.

but i hate to see the body i've abused.

~~this is what happened~~

this is what i learned

there was a poem here
that i wrote out of spite
because that was the only way
i knew how to write.

but i realize now
that by dragging these chains
and passing the blame,
that i had nothing to gain
by noticing i was doing just the same
as the people who i thought had created
my pain.

to be the bigger person
is to embrace the power of grace,
and
instead of tearing others apart,
never forget, but find forgiveness in your heart.

and recognize that those problems that have grown
were started in the fields that only you own.

so instead of telling you
"this is what happened"
between myself and someone i trusted,
i would rather tell you about
'this is what i learned"
when i grew and adjusted.

i am imperfect
but i am learning.

i am learning how to forgive
and how to create
art that isn't fueled by hate.
i am learning how to love
and how to be loved
the way i deserve to be.

i am learning how to surround myself
with all things
peaceful
light
bright
and learning that the only way i can be happy
is simply learning how imporant it is
to be me.

and i am learning
that there is so much beauty
in the pain
that is learning.

a list of broken things

i cannot think of broken things
because the two halves of my heart
taught themselves to beat
as if they were one,
and because the record
that reminds me of you
has always been scratched,
and because the words
from my pens
always end up burned,
and because the spirit
someone borrowed from me,
was brought back torn,
and because the words they said to me
are still stuck
in only places i can see.

so i cannot think of broken things
because broken has always been
my normalcy.

#ad

"HEART FOR SALE"
"name your price
older model, used, but runs okay
issues with (t)rust
a few broken pieces, but those can be bought
will probably be thrown away if a home is not found."

i wouldn't buy it
either.

evening gown

in the moonlight,
the ocean looks like
the sequined fabric of a beautiful
evening gown.

so maybe if i jump into it
and envelope myself
in rhinestone-silk like the stars,
people will finally think that
i am beautiful.

is it me?

sometimes i can't tell
if they're laughing a joke someone told.
or at me,
and the way i'm dressed
and the fact that i've gained weight
so my skin is breaking out.

or if the laughter is just in my head
because i don't even know
who those people are.

the second floor study lounge

there were nights where my mattress felt more like a bed of nails than memory foam, and where the air became too thick to breathe as tension filled my lungs with toxic thoughts that chocked me out. so i ran out of the basement, out of my room, to breathe.

and as i gasped for air, i looked up to see the sunrise peek over the mountains and a view i never saw from my room. it was if the sky was saying hello. and i saw those cotton candy clouds float through the sky as the birds sung morning lullabies.

so i sat down, in the second floor study lounge, and watched the sky.

i could breathe again as the sun jumped over the mountains and the sky grew blue. and i breathed until the sun became the moon and the clouds became stars.

and at night, as i laid back on my bed of nails, with the thick air filling my lungs, i asked myself why the sky was more beautiful elsewhere.

i was the one who fought

i lost sleep
during the nights i spent drowning in saltwater,
diving in memories
of a simpler summer.

and during these nights
i sent you messages while you slept,
and they were marinated in regret
and sprinked with the desire to be yours
while my tears dropped onto my keyboard,
begging for you back
while you slept.

you left me again, too.
three days before i turned another decade
and i didn't even need to blow out the candles,
saltwater stifles flames just as well.
but i still wrote you messages
asking for the forgiveness i didn't need in the first place
while your phone was turned off.

i was the one who swam in saltwater,
who wrote you words of love
that i didn't even spare to give to myself,
who begged for you to stay
when i was the one who had reasons to leave.

i was the one who fought
while you slept.

so when will i get to rest?

ghost

a floating sheet:
my inpenetrable alias.

i am a ghost.

i stay silent and observe
never intervening, and never heard.
visible to only those who search for me,
if they ever do at all.
so
i stay away, far into the
background as i wonder , "will anyone
look for me
even though i am long gone
?

empath, kind of.

i feel too much
but i show it too little
until i feel as little
as i show it.

lost and found

she lost who she was
so she searched
in the judgmental eyes
and sharp, cutting tongues and the
hollow words of others who told her
this was who she was meant to be.

and she searched
in the strong, stomach curdling waters
of glass bottles that promised a message and in the
thick smoke she pretended to inhale,
and in rooms full of people
that made her feel alone.

but if she had only searched
in the tattooed arms of familiarity
and the soft country melodies
of home.

and if she had only searched
in the dog-eared chapters of green tea stained books and in the
chords of an out of tune piano and in
films shot in black and white and in
socks that hit just above the knee,
and in clay covered fingers
moving frame by frame.

but that's okay,
because i know that eventually
she'll look in the mirror,
smiling,
and find me again.

open window

i like to sleep with the windows open,
but especially when it storms.
because then i can hear the winds
whispering to me,
"tomorrow will be brighter."

my biggest life lesson

friends can break your heart too.

even the ones who thought were truly true.

a world without you

a world without you
has cloud covered skies that are
grey instead of blue.

i wish you still looked at me.

i wish you still looked at me the way you did when you saw me first: the girl with big glasses and an even bigger book in front of her; the girl who was "different" from other girls but didn't know it; the girl you knew nothing about but somehow knew everything you needed to know.

i wished you still looked at me with starry eyes and through rose-colored glasses.

i just wished you still *looked* at me.

3.5.20

my heart aches when i think of a world
without your laugh
as the melody in every song i hear.

cloud

i am just a cloud,
a smudge on an otherwise
perfecly blue sky.

midnight thoughts.

i just want to be
in your tattooed arms again:
they're my safety net.

dear universe

let me fall in love
with the golden fireworks
and the twinkling stars
that dance and glow above me
every night.

let me fall in love
with waking up to those ocean waves,
and the way the sun
kisses my skin.

let me fall in love
with the moments too short to capture
and the people
i will only meet once.

let me fall in love
with laughter
with light
with happiness
with mistakes
with pain
with loss
with forgiveness.

let me fall in love
with life.

for los angeles

i live in the city of angels,
the land of palm tree painted skies.
sunsets, orange like the sweet, juicy fruit,
and red like the tails of devils.
i swim in the waters that are the perfect shade of blue,
and walk in city streets where the lights never seem to turn off.

but then i saw the lights turn from bright, to dim, to off,
and the streets were dark like the abandoned halos of angels.
the sun's golden haze was replaced by storm clouds of dark blue,
and thick smoke from glowing fires clouded my serene skies.
those city streets filled my mind with a thousand devils
begging me to try their forbidden fruit.

and with each bite of that fruit,
i felt a light inside of me turn from bright, to dim, to off.
the illusion of the angels in my city turned to that of devils,
and i watched my sanity fly away on the wings of my angels.
the more i stared at the superficial, perfect skies,
i grew to hate the color blue.

how are you supposed to stay sane under a sky that's always blue?
or in a garden where every tree bears the same fruit?
i stared at palm trees every day and begged them for new skies,
and prayed for those lights to turn back on, yet they stayed off
as i lived in the city of angels,
surrounded by devils.

i cowered in fear of those devils
and felt nothing but blue.
yet at night i cried to my angels
as i stuck my fingers down my throat to surrender the forbidden fruit,
that i hated that the lights were off
and i hated the city known for blue skies.

but then i decided to change, and so did the skies,
as i fought back against the devils
and switched my light to on from off.
i swam in the ocean again and learned to love blue,
and looked for gardens that grew different fruit.
and i felt world glow like the halos on my angels.

i take pictures of the skies
when they're grey, orange, and especially blue.

i ignore the city's devils,
i think i'm allergic to their fruit.

and i think it's beautiful how the lights never seem to turn off
in the city of angels.

the view from the moon

across from my bed
on a wall in my room
is a mural of the earth
as the view from the moon.

sometimes, if i concentrate hard enough,
its almost like i'm there.
surrounded by stars from other worlds
that shoot and grant wishes if i continue to stare.

and i notice that from here
the earth is so small
and i wonder if people know i'm in space
or if they even care at all.

i wonder if they can hear my stomach growl
the way it has been all day
and i wonder if someone will ask "are you hungry?"
or, better yet, "are you okay?"

and i wonder if they can look at my eyes,
puffy and red from a sleepless night,
and hold me and tell me,
"you're gonna be alright."

i wonder if they can see me cry,
and the way i scratch and i shake
and the way i can hide it all
just for someone else's sake.

and as i sit on the moon
staring at the planet i claim is my home
i find myself realizing:
that's where i feel most alone.

but for some reason, i choose to open my eyes,
and take a look around the moon to see
someone else who is crying for help,
someone like me.

i realize
i am not the only one on the moon.

i am not the only one wishing on shooting stars.
i am not the only one with puffy, red eyes
and anxiety attacks
and a body i despise.

i am not the only one
who feels like the earth is not my home,
for on the moon it seems like everyone
feels just as alone.

and suddenly, i'm no longer in space,
but rather, laying in my bed,
realizing that my journey to the stars
was all in my head.

space was just that mural
on that wall in my room,
and you are not the only one who is looking at the earth
as the view from the moon.

growth.

my arms hurt
because i used them to push myself back up.
my legs ache
because it's been months since i've walked.
and my head is throbbing
because the soil of life has been weighing on it for so long.

but
my eyes are relearning to see,
my fingers are relearning to feel,
my throat is finding its voice,
my heart is starting to beat again.

it hurts
and it's hard
but damn,
i forgot how good it feels to grow.

when i feel understood

- empty coffee shops with folk song soundtracks
- in a car listening to *space oddity*, only surrounded by the stars and night sky
- on the ruled lines of a notebook
- as i write this.
- my apartment while it's raining (with the windows open)
- bookstores
- watching movies where characters go to space
- next to him, watching cooking shows with cheap tacos, hold the lettuce
- on film sets handing out hot coffee
- swimming in the ocean on a sunny day in november

mantra

i am stronger than
sticks and stones and
broken bones,
and i am stronger than
bruised betrayal and loveless lies.

i am stronger than
the hills of hurt, and the
peaks of pain, and the
seas of sadness.

i am stronger
than the things that keep me under.

and so are you.

when i'm with you, i feel like i'm stargazing

i want to tell you everything
while we lay under blankets
and use eachother from warmth
while you trace my skin like paper,
connecting my freckles like constellations,
looking at me with stars in your eyes.

i want to tell you how
nobody has ever looked at me
the way you just did,
the way ancient astronomers looked at the milky way
for the very first time,
or the way astronauts look at the earth
while walking on the moon.

and when i'm with you,
i feel like i'm stargazing.

and i just wanted to tell you that.

sea salt songs

when i feel lost
i sit on the rocks lining the ocean,
close my eyes,
and listen to the way the sea salt scented breeze
sings songs through my hair,
curating an oceanic symphony that only i can hear.

and i listen to it until my clothes smell like the pacific
and until the sun dips below the current,
bringing my music to a pause.

i long to close my eyes for just a little longer
and sink further into mother nature's embrace,
for it is in the sea salt songs of the ocean
where i finally feel found.

word vomit: m.r & j.j

we mocked being young and stupid because it's weird to admit that you want to be sixteen again and we knew that...so we did all of the things young souls do, and made fun of them for being cliché and dumb while laughing over shitty chinese food and singing along to some song from the credits of some movie inside of a car with all of the windows down on a neon-lit freeway speckled in stars because we thought it was funny and ironic, but the only ironic thing about it was that we felt joy in the cliché and in the ironic because we realized that the three of us had been the very thing we were mocking all along.

perfection

her arms are a scratching post
for sabotaging thoughts
and harsh words.

her mind is full of paths
she never intended to pave,
nor did she ever even want to.

she didn't ask for raw arms
and a labyrinth mind.

she only asked to feel normal.
but little did she know
her imperfections
are perfections.

you are celestial

let me trace your tattoos
the same way the ancient greeks drew constellations.

we're both touching stars.

west virginia

my best friend texted me one day and said "we should go see the world's largest teapot." and, of course, i said "yes" because who wouldn't want to see the world's largest teapot in chester, west virginia?

so we drove across state lines (un)ironically listening to county music because we thought it would make us "blend in" better with our surroundings when it only made us stick out more, but we didn't care.

kind of in the same way that *i* didn't care whenever we pulled up to the world's largest teapot and we saw that it actually wasn't large at all and that it was on the side of the road and in order to see it, we had to park at a run-down gas station that had advertisements for catfish tournaments and a surplus of pickup trucks out front.

and after some shitty self-timer photos and going to (probably) the only taco bell within a 100 mile radius of chester, west virginia, we drove home laughing about how stupid we were to drive 40 minutes to something just to make fun of it for only 10.

but we also knew that there was nobody else in the entire world that we would ever want to do that with but each other.

self pity

i spent so much time
swimming in tears
that i forgot how good
the sunlight feels.

tiger stripes

those marks on your body
are not imperfections.

they are
ocean waves:
ripples of femininity and grace.
tiger stripes,
and beautiful scars that remind you of what it means
to be a woman.

weather

don't apologize
for the way the wind may blow,
it's just the weather.

orange, ca skies

i've been thinking alot about the sky and about the song "sheep" by mt. joy because of the way both of those things make me feel.

i think about how the sky is different every place i go. how the sunsets on the east coast are more pink than the west and the way that the sky is a different shade of blue in every city that i've been to. and i think about how, sometimes, i feel connected to the sky in some kind of inexplainable way that *i* can't even explain.

there's something beautiful about that. there's something beautiful about how the sky never looks the same. there's something so undeniably beautiful about how the sky is always changing because i guess that reminds me that i have the capability to do the same.

i want to live to see more skies and marvel at how, sometimes, even the skies on the west coast can be just as pink as the east and smile because i feel more at home than i ever have before here

jake

messy hair and tattoos,
thick glasses and hooded sweatshirts,
kind words and soft touches,
fresh cologne and mint gum:
i ask myself what i did
to deserve my senses
to be filled by you.

word vomit: c.g

my apartment was a mess, but you came over anyway and ate burnt french toast and frozen breakfast sausages as you aired your wounds at my kitchen table and seasoned your food with salty tears, but after they dried you sat on my floor and did homework beside me and thanked me for being there while you broke down...but what you didn't know was that i was breaking down too, and in making subpar breakfast for you, and watching cartoons and painting with cheap watercolors and procrastinating essays with you, you aided my breakdown without even knowing it, just by being there.

the soundtrack of my life

the soundtrack of my life
consists of
melodies of laughter
mixed with the complex lyrics of an argument
and love poems.

and the bass booms
with the crashing newport beach waves
and fireworks on summer nights.

excitement induced ska-punk,
crying acoustic guitars,
sunshine-filled rap beats,
all with the underlying synth
of justified, joyful stupidity.

press play to live.

for you

i write poems for me
and people like me:
who feel alone in rooms full of people.
who feel lost while holding an idealistic map.
who feel sadness behind a joyful masquerade.

i see you.
and i understand what it feels like
to wear a smile that isn't yours,
to live a life you don't feel is yours,
and tending to everyone's happiness
but your own.

you are not alone.
and because of you,
neither am i.

ben's house

trampolines are usually for jumping
but tonight we can use them
to connect stars into incorrect constellations
and wonder if this is the last time
we'll ever be breathing the same
smoke-scented air ever again.

i love you.

please, just keep going.
for me, for you, and for those
who have stopped running.

word vomit: a.h.

we went to the beach at midnight because you came into my room and said "let's go," so we did, and i dipped my toes into the sharp black waters and ran in the sand even though it cut up my feet, and i smiled bigger than i had in a long time even though my body was freezing and i lost my socks...it didn't matter because, with you, i felt the warmth of friendship and i realized that the coldness of life could never freeze me as long as you are there.

eye-tag

you close your eyes
but i open mine,
just so i can catch a glimpse
of what contentment looks like.

and you laugh, and roll over and tell me to rest,
and that you're tired from all of the running around
that you do.
but i'll wait for you with open eyes, because i love playing
eye-tag with you.

hometown hero

driving down back roads
is the closest i've felt to
flying in so long.

daydreamer

in an unmade bed,
she listens to acoustic love songs
as she reads off of the dog-eared,
water-damaged, and wrinkled pages of a book she never finishes,
because she hates when
things end.

and she daydreams of laughter in lavender fields
and salty, seawater smiles
as if she were the muse of those words
on those pages, and as if she lived in those worlds
that she created.

her head in the clouds,
her feet in mismatched socks.

give her some time to daydream
before bringing her back to earth.

starry eyed

you make me write about stars and the moon and constellations and orbits and the sun and all things far out of this world.

you are my solar system.

the last day of summer

the sunsets fall faster
whenever summer comes to a close,
but at least the sky is still beautiful
for those last fleeting moments.

and i all i want to do
is hold on to the sunset
and its ribbons of pink and blue
and hold onto the way that this summer has made me feel
for just a little bit longer.

"please just don't
s l i p
through my fingers."

i say as the summer
lets
me
go.

brooke, a haiku for u

you are all things bright:
sunlight, baby blue, car rides
adventures and smiles.

gran

i know you'll live on
in all the orchid petals
that will garden.

and i know that those flowers
will bloom the most beautiful.

pinkies

i pinky promise
that i'll still write you poems
when my pen runs dry.

self-affirmations

i am all things.
yellow, clouds,
birds that chirp.
music with drums,
the taste of cherry coke
on a parched tongue.

i am all things good.

i could go on forever

there aren't enough pages in this book
to express how i feel about you.

i hope a few poems were good enough.

moon phases

i've grown up and realized that we're a lot like the moon: sometimes, we need to feel emptiness to remember the beauty of being full again.

before the shower thoughts: part two

i know now why i look at myself before i shower. i like to see the way the curly pieces of my hair frame my face right after i take my hair down. i like to see the way my stomach looks like it's smiling after i eat my favorite meal. i like to see the way my hips sway while i sing my favorite song into my hairbrush, and the way my body flows effortlessly like the water from the faucet. i like to see the way my ass looks in different, model-eque poses and the way my smile lights up when i finally feel like a cover girl.

i like to see the way my skin is healing from pinches and red blotches. i like to see the same reflection in the mirror as yesterday without it changing before my eyes. i like to see the uncontrollable things i've been taught to despise and the thousands of things i've learned to love and the thousands more i will in time.

i like to see the body i love.

and i love to see the body that's mine.

asleep

i like to pretend that i am
asleep
whenever i lie beside you.
because, unlike whenever i'm dreaming,
i can still feel the love
radiating from the oceans of your eyes,
and the golden sparks of affection
glowing from your fingertips.

i can feel your hands
getting lost in the knotted jungle
of my hair,
methodically weaving their way
through the jumbled maze,
careful not to wake me.

i can feel your lips
planting butterflies on my forehead,
like some sort of secret message
for when i wake up.

but i am awake,
as i make sure my lips
are puckered in a perfect sleeping pout
so you don't see how i drool.
and how i make sure
my eyes are rested lightly,
and my breathing steady
because sleeping beauty would never snore.

i'm awake as you whisper
goodnight
and as you doze off
into your dreams
and as you think that i'm doing
just the same.

and that's probably why
i'm constantly sleepy
whenever i'm with you.

the girl who lived.

she smells like bonfires
and stale taco bell
with a hint of cheap tequila
mixed with printer-ink covered needles
and spotty stick-and-poke tattoos.

and the makeup she spent 45 minutes on is melting away
and her mascara and flaked and smudged
with both sweat and tears
of laughter she spilt over
gasping conversations and fits of pure joy.

she may not look the best
but inside she feels beautiful:
her sadness is overpowered by the
endorphins that friendship provide
and the music of the local classic rock station.

for the first time in a long time
she is living.

a genuine smile from ear to ear
surrounded by people who are eager to hear
her stories and trials and terrible jokes.
all at once, she is complete:
surrounded by people who love life
as much as they are loved by her.

these people make her want to live another day
and for the first time in years, she wants to stay
on the earth that has been so cruel.
because, despite the bad,
there is so much she has yet to write about,
and so many more ink markings she has yet to collect,
and so many more laughs she has yet to bellow,
and so many more times she has yet to watch
the sun both set and rise in the same day.

and although she may be broken,
for just a few joyful hours,
she feels as if she had never been battered
in the first place.

for she is the girl who lived
without realizing that she has been living
all along.

afterword.

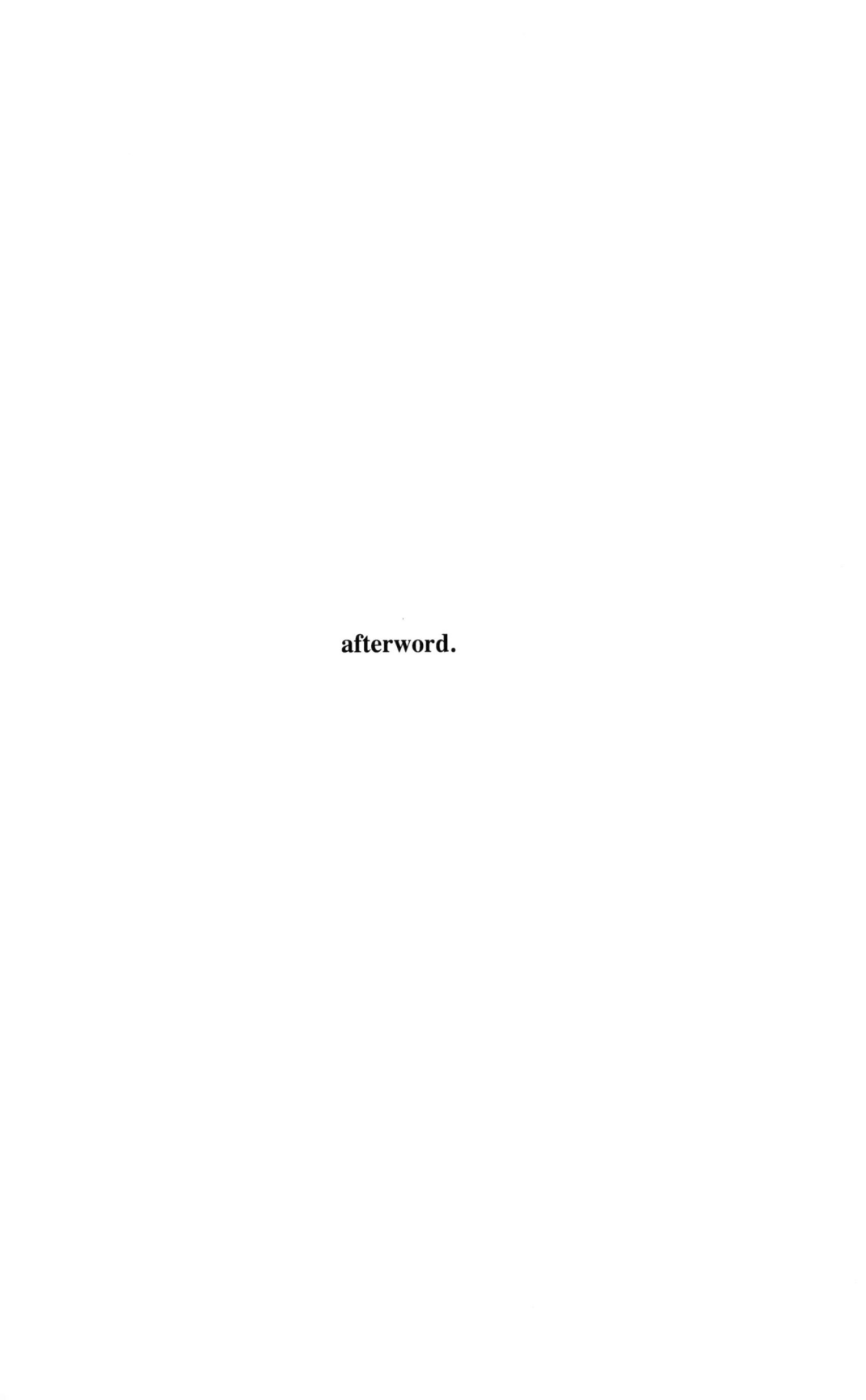

i think that anyone who has ever met me knows that i have a deep, irrational fear of being made a fool. even deeper, i am terrfied of failure. i hate losing, i hate feeling like the butt of a joke, and i hate disappointing those around me...even if it's just me dropping a stuffed animal at the last second on the claw machine.

so, with that being said, the thought of self-publishing a collection of poetry, that i wrote during some of the darkest times of my life, was probably the most anxiety-inducing and terrifying thing i could ever do. i'm a people pleaser, a person with a lot of walls that only serve to guard my emotions so they don't become a burden to others. and putting my most vulnerable self out on display for the whole world, subjecting myself to the possibility of rejection or scrutiny or failure...now *that's* a real life nightmare.

i've been writing poetry for as long as i can remember. in fact, people used to pay me in high school english class to write their poetry assignments for them. and as i continued to write, the more i became comfortable finding a style of poetry that reflected who i was in words.

when i moved across the county to california, i met a lot of new people and was fully engulfed into a completely different world. living near los angeles was so different than my humble, rural-suburban town in the midwest. the food was different, the nightlife was different, and the people were certainly different.

i felt, somehow, as if i were on the moon. i felt alone and alienated. and it felt like people on earth didn't notice my struggles because i was so far away and because they had this mindset that the moon was as beautiful as it looked and that just wasn't the case.

it's hard to feel that way. and it can feel like that the only way you could ever be able to feel. but being alone forces you to grow in ways you never thought possible. through sadness, pain, and heartbreak, i learned so much about myself and realized that there are so many people that felt the same way i did.
thorugh all of the bad (and there was quite a lot), i had the ability to find myself again and force myself out of a comfort zone i was so used to.

i have a long way to go, the moon is pretty far away from the earth. but i'm learning how to find my way home and i think there's something really beautiful about that.

i'll be okay. we'll be okay. i'm sure of it.

acknowledgements.

thank you to my amazing parents and family for supporting me always: mom, dad, johnny, and zach. from my high school mood swings and endless crying, your constant encouragement is part of the reason why this hunk of paper exists. and i am so, so, so grateful for that. also, thank you for just being the coolest. i don't tell you that enough.

thank you to the inspirations behind these poems: good and bad.

thank you to my person, jake. i have never met someone who inspires so many words, yet so much writer's block.

thank you to my best friends: brooke, sydney, sammie, sombre, indie, and kayleigh. i remember letting you read my poems at lunch in high school and in study hall in middle school. i am so grateful for your constant love and support in everything i do. i wouldn't trade you all for the world.

thank you to abby, steve, ben, clarisse, matt, jason, pete, mckenna, brenna, gianna, claire, sina, davis, kaila, jen, and to any other special people who have supported me.

and most of all, thank you. whether i reach an audience of 10, or 10,000,000, i will be forever grateful that my words are helping someone. anyone. thank you for making me feel less alone by making you feel less alone. you will never know how much gratitude i feel toward you for giving this little, emo book a home. i am so glad you are here. thank you. thank you. thank you.

i'll catch you all on the flipside.

keep up with me!

instagram: @juliannammarie
twitter: @juliannamariem
pinterest: @itsjuliannamarie
website: juliannamarie.co

for inquires, commissions, and collaborations:
julianna@juliannamarie.co

Printed in Great Britain
by Amazon